I0620999

THE RELUCTANT HEROES

Start Publishing PD LLC
Copyright © 2024 by Start Publishing PD LLC

All rights reserved, including the right to reproduce this book or portions thereof in any form whatsoever.

Start Publishing PD is a registered trademark of Start Publishing PD LLC
Manufactured in the United States of America

Cover art: Shutterstock/Taisiya Kozorez

Cover design: Jennifer Do

10 9 8 7 6 5 4 3 2 1

ISBN 979-8-8809-1975-8

THE RELUCTANT HEROES

by Frank M. Robinson

Pioneers have always resented their wanderlust, hated their hardships. But the future brings a new grudge—when pioneers stay put and scholars do the exploring!

*

The very young man sat on the edge of the sofa and looked nervous. He carefully studied his fingernails and ran his hands through his hair and picked imaginary lint off the upholstery.

"I have a chance to go with the first research expedition to Venus," he said.

The older man studied the very young man thoughtfully and then leaned over to his humidor and offered him a cigaret. "It's nice to have the new air units now. There was a time when we had to be very careful about things like smoking."

The very young man was annoyed.

"I don't think I want to go," he blurted. "I don't think I would care to spend two years there."

The older man blew a smoke ring and watched it drift toward the air exhaust vent.

"You mean you would miss it here, the people you've known and grown up with, the little familiar things that have made up your life here. You're afraid the glamor would wear off and you would get to hate it on Venus."

The very young man nodded miserably. "I guess that's it."

"Anything else?"

The very young man found his fingernails extremely fascinating again and finally said, in a low voice, "Yes, there is."

"A girl?"

A nod confirmed this.

It was the older man's turn to look thoughtful. "You know, I'm sure, that psychologists and research men agree that research stations should be staffed by couples. That is, of course, as soon as it's practical."

"But that might be a long time!" the very young man protested.

4

THE RELUCTANT HEROES

"It might be—but sometimes it's sooner than you think. And the goal is worth it."

"I suppose so, but—"

The older man smiled. "Still the reluctant heroes," he said, somewhat to himself.

*

Chapman stared at the radio key.

Three years on the Moon and they didn't want him to come back.

Three years on the Moon and they thought he'd be glad to stay for more. Just raise his salary or give him a bonus, the every-man-has-his-price idea. They probably thought he liked it there.

Oh, sure, he loved it. Canned coffee, canned beans, canned pills, and canned air until your insides felt as though they were plated with tin. Life in a cramped, smelly little hut where you could take only ten steps in any one direction. Their little scientific home of tomorrow with none of the modern conveniences, a charming place where you couldn't take a shower, couldn't brush your teeth, and your kidneys didn't work right.

And for double his salary they thought he'd be glad to stay for another year and a half. Or maybe three. He should probably be glad he had the opportunity.

The key started to stutter again, demanding an answer.

He tapped out his reply: "No!"

There was a silence and then the key stammered once more in a sudden fit of bureaucratic rage. Chapman stuffed a rag under it and ignored it. He turned to the hammocks, strung against the bulkhead on the other side of the room.

The chattering of the key hadn't awakened anybody; they were still asleep, making the animal noises that people usually make in slumber. Dowden, half in the bottom hammock and half on the floor, was snoring peacefully. Dahl, the poor kid who was due for stopover, was mumbling to himself. Julius Klein, with that look of ineffable happiness on his face, looked as if he had just squirmed under the tent to his personal idea of heaven. Donley and Bening were lying perfectly still, their covers not mussed, sleeping very lightly.

Lord, Chapman thought, I'll be happy when I can see some other faces.

"What'd they want?" Klein had one eyelid open and a questioning look on his face.

"They wanted me to stay until the next relief ship lands," Chapman whispered back.

"What did you say?"

He shrugged. "No."

"You kept it short," somebody else whispered. It was Donley, up and sitting on the side of his hammock. "If it had been me, I would have told them just what they could do about it."

*

The others were awake now, with the exception of Dahl who had his face to the bulkhead and a pillow over his head.

Dowden rubbed his eyes sleepily. "Sore, aren't you?"

"Kind of. Who wouldn't be?"

"Well, don't let it throw you. They've never been here on the Moon. They don't know what it's like. All they're trying to do is get a good man to stay on the job a while longer."

"*All* they're trying to do," Chapman said sarcastically. "They've got a fat chance."

"They think you've found a home here," Donley said.

"Why the hell don't you guys shut up until morning?" Dahl was awake, looking bitter. "Some of us still have to stay here, you know. Some of us aren't going back today."

No, Chapman thought, some of us aren't going back. You aren't. And Dixon's staying, too. Only Dixon isn't ever going back.

6

THE RELUCTANT HEROES

Klein jerked his thumb toward Dahl's bunk, held a finger to his lips, and walked noiselessly over to the small electric stove. It was his day for breakfast duty.

The others started lacing up their bunks, getting ready for their last day of work on the Moon. In a few hours they'd be relieved by members of the Third research group and they'd be on their way back to Earth.

And that includes me, Chapman thought. I'm going home. I'm finally going home.

He walked silently to the one small, quartz window in the room. It was morning—the Moon's "morning"—and he shivered slightly. The rays of the Sun were just striking the far rim of the crater and long shadows shot across the crater floor. The rest of it was still blanketed in a dark jumble of powdery pumice and jagged peaks that would make the Black Hills of Dakota look like paradise.

A hundred yards from the research bunker he could make out the small mound of stones and the forlorn homemade cross, jury-rigged out of small condensed milk tins slid over crossed iron bars. You could still see the footprints in the powdery soil where the group had gathered about the grave. It had been more than eighteen months ago, but there was no wind to wear those tracks away. They'd be there forever.

That's what happened to guys like Dixon, Chapman thought. On the Moon, one mistake could use up your whole quota of chances.

Klein came back with the coffee. Chapman took a cup, gagged, and forced himself to swallow the rest of it. It had been in the can for so long you could almost taste the glue on the label.

*

Donley was warming himself over his cup, looking thoughtful. Dowden and Bening were struggling into their suits, getting

7

ready to go outside. Dahl was still sitting on his hammock, trying to ignore them.

"Think we ought to radio the space station and see if they've left there yet?" Klein asked.

"I talked to them on the last call," Chapman said. "The relief ship left there twelve hours ago. They should get here"—he looked at his watch—"in about six and a half hours."

"Chap, you know, I've been thinking," Donley said quietly. "You've been here just twice as long as the rest of us. What's the first thing you're going to do once you get back?"

It hit them, then. Dowden and Bening looked blank for a minute and blindly found packing cases to sit on. The top halves of their suits were still hanging on the bulkhead. Klein lowered his coffee cup and looked grave. Even Dahl glanced up expectantly.

"I don't know," Chapman said slowly. "I guess I was trying not to think of that. I suppose none of us have. We've been like little kids who have waited so long for Christmas that they just can't believe it when it's finally Christmas Eve."

Klein nodded in agreement. "I haven't been here three years like you have, but I think I know what you mean." He warmed up to it as the idea sank in. "Just what the hell *are* you going to do?"

"Nothing very spectacular," Chapman said, smiling. "I'm going to rent a room over Times Square, get a recording of a rikky-tik piano, and drink and listen to the music and watch the people on the street below. Then I think I'll see somebody."

"Who's the somebody?" Donley asked.

Chapman grinned. "Oh, just somebody. What are you going to do, Dick?"

"Well, I'm going to do something practical. First of all, I want to turn over all my geological samples to the government. Then I'm going to sell my life story to the movies and then—why,

THE RELUCTANT HEROES

then, I think I'll get drunk!"

Everybody laughed and Chapman turned to Klein.

"How about you, Julius?"

Klein looked solemn. "Like Dick, I'll first get rid of my obligations to the expedition. Then I think I'll go home and see my wife."

They were quiet. "I thought all members of the groups were supposed to be single," Donley said.

"They are. And I can see their reasons for it. But who could pass up the money the Commission was paying?"

"If I had to do it all over again? Me," said Donley promptly.

They laughed. Somebody said: "Go play your record, Chap. Today's the day for it."

The phonograph was a small, wind-up model that Chapman had smuggled in when he had landed with the First group. The record was old and the shellac was nearly worn off, but the music was good.

Way Back Home by Al Lewis.

*

They ran through it twice. They were beginning to feel it now, Chapman thought. They were going to go home in a little while and the idea was just starting to sink in.

"You know, Chap," Donley said, "it won't seem like the same old Moon without you on it. Why, we'll look at it when we're out spooning or something and it just won't have the same old appeal."

"Like they say in the army," Bening said, "you never had it so good. You found a home here."

The others chimed in and Chapman grinned. Yesterday or a week ago they couldn't have done it. He had been there too long and he had hated it too much.

The party quieted down after a while and Dowden and Bening finished getting into their suits. They still had a section of the

9

sky to map before they left. Donley was right after them. There was an outcropping of rock that he wanted a sample of and some strata he wished to investigate.

And the time went faster when you kept busy.

Chapman stopped them at the lock. "Remember to check your suits for leaks," he warned. "And check the valves of your oxygen tanks."

Donley looked sour. "I've gone out at least five hundred times," he said, "and you check me each time."

"And I'd check you five hundred more," Chapman said. "It takes only one mistake. And watch out for blisters under the pumice crust. You go through one of those and that's it, brother."

Donley sighed. "Chap, you watch us like an old mother hen. You see we check our suits, you settle our arguments, you see that we're not bored and that we stay healthy and happy. I think you'd blow our noses for us if we caught cold. But some day, Chap old man, you're gonna find out that your little boys can watch out for themselves!"

But he checked his suit for leaks and tested the valve of his tank before he left.

Only Klein and Chapman were left in the bunker. Klein was at the work table, carefully labeling some lichen specimens.

"I never knew you were married," Chapman said.

Klein didn't look up. "There wasn't much sense in talking about it. You just get to thinking and wanting—and there's nothing you can do about it. You talk about it and it just makes it worse."

"She let you go without any fuss, huh?"

"No, she didn't make any fuss. But I don't think she liked to see me go, either." He laughed a little. "At least I hope she didn't."

*

THE RELUCTANT HEROES

They were silent for a while. "What do you miss most, Chap?" Klein asked. "Oh, I know what we said a little while ago, but I mean seriously."

Chapman thought a minute. "I think I miss the sky," he said quietly. "The blue sky and the green grass and trees with leaves on them that turn color in the Fall. I think, when I go back, that I'd like to go out in a rain storm and strip and feel the rain on my skin."

He stopped, feeling embarrassed. Klein's expression was encouraging. "And then I think I'd like to go downtown and just watch the shoppers on the sidewalks. Or maybe go to a burlesque house and smell the cheap perfume and the popcorn and the people sweating in the dark."

He studied his hands. "I think what I miss most is people—all kinds of people. Bad people and good people and fat people and thin people, and people I can't understand. People who wouldn't know an atom from an artichoke. And people who wouldn't give a damn. We're a quarter of a million miles from nowhere, Julius, and to make it literary, I think I miss my fellow man more than anything."

"Got a girl back home?" Klein asked almost casually.

"Yes."

"You're not like Dahl. You've never mentioned it."

"Same reason you didn't mention your wife. You get to thinking about it."

Klein flipped the lid on the specimen box. "Going to get married when you get back?"

Chapman was at the port again, staring out at the bleak landscape. "We hope to."

"Settle down in a small cottage and raise lots of little Chapmans, eh?"

Chapman nodded.

"That's the only future," Klein said.

He put away the box and came over to the port. Chapman moved over so they both could look out.

"Chap." Klein hesitated a moment. "What happened to Dixon?"

"He died," Chapman said. "He was a good kid, all wrapped up in science. Being on the Moon was the opportunity of a lifetime. He thought so much about it that he forgot a lot of little things—like how to stay alive. The day before the Second group came, he went out to finish some work he was interested in. He forgot to check for leaks and whether or not the valve on his tank was all the way closed. We couldn't get to him in time."

"He had his walkie-talkie with him?"

"Yes. It worked fine, too. We heard everything that went through his mind at the end."

Klein's face was blank. "What's your real job here, Chap? Why does somebody have to stay for stopover?"

"Hell, lots of reasons, Julius. You can't get a whole relief crew and let them take over cold. They have to know where you left off. They have to know where things are, how things work, what to watch out for. And then, because you've been here a year and a half and know the ropes, you have to watch them to see that they stay alive in spite of themselves. The Moon's a new environment and you have to learn how to live in it. There's a lot of things to learn—and some people just never learn."

"You're nursemaid, then."

"I suppose you could call it that."

*

Klein said, "You're not a scientist, are you?"

"No, you should know that. I came as the pilot of the first ship. We made the bunker out of parts of the ship so there wasn't anything to go back on. I'm a good mechanic and I made

THE RELUCTANT HEROES

myself useful with the machinery. When it occurred to us that somebody was going to have to stay over, I volunteered. I thought the others were so important that it was better they should take their samples and data back to Earth when the first relief ship came."

"You wouldn't do it again, though, would you?"

"No, I wouldn't."

"Do you think Dahl will do as good a job as you've done here?"

Chapman frowned. "Frankly, I hadn't thought of that. I don't believe I care. I've put in my time; it's somebody else's turn now. He volunteered for it. I think I was fair in explaining all about the job when you talked it over among yourselves."

"You did, but I don't think Dahl's the man for it. He's too young, too much of a kid. He volunteered because he thought it made him look like a hero. He doesn't have the judgment that an older man would have. That you have."

Chapman turned slowly around and faced Klein.

"I'm not the indispensable man," he said slowly, "and even if I was, it wouldn't make any difference to me. I'm sorry if Dahl is young. So was I. I've lost three years up here. And I don't intend to lose any more."

Klein held up his hands. "Look, Chap, I didn't mean you should stay. I know how much you hate it and the time you put in up here. It's just—" His voice trailed away. "It's just that I think it's such a damn important job."

Klein had gone out in a last search for rock lichens and Chapman enjoyed one of his relatively few moments of privacy. He wandered over to his bunk and opened his barracks bag. He checked the underwear and his toothbrush and shaving kit for maybe the hundredth time and pushed the clothing down farther in the canvas. It was foolish because the bag was already packed and had been for a week. He remembered stalling it off for as long as he could and then the quiet satisfaction about a week before, when he had opened his small gear locker and transferred its meager belongings to the bag.

He hadn't actually needed to pack, of course. In less than twenty-four hours he'd be back on Earth where he could drown himself in toothpaste and buy more tee shirts than he could wear in a lifetime. He could leave behind his shorts and socks and the outsize shirts he had inherited from—who was it? Driesbach?—of the First group. Dahl could probably use them or maybe one of the boys in the Third.

*

But it wasn't like going home unless you packed. It was part of the ritual, like marking off the last three weeks in pencil on the gray steel of the bulkhead beside his hammock. Just a few hours ago, when he woke up, he had made the last check mark and signed his name and the date. His signature was right beneath Dixon's.

He frowned when he thought of Dixon and slid back the catch on the top of the bag and locked it. They should never have sent a kid like Dixon to the Moon.

He had just locked the bag when he heard the rumble of the airlock and the soft hiss of air. Somebody had come back earlier than expected. He watched the inner door swing open and the spacesuited figure clump in and unscrew its helmet.

Dahl. He had gone out to help Dowden on the Schmidt telescope. Maybe Dowden hadn't needed any help, with Bening along. Or more likely, considering the circumstances, Dahl wasn't much good at helping anybody today.

Dahl stripped off his suit. His face was covered with light beads of sweat and his eyes were frightened.

He moistened his lips slightly. "Do—do you think they'll ever have relief ships up here more often than every eighteen months, Chap? I mean, considering the advance of—"

THE RELUCTANT HEROES

"No," Chapman interrupted bluntly. "I don't. Not at least for ten years. The fuel's too expensive and the trip's too hazardous. On freight charges alone you're worth your weight in platinum when they send you here. Even if it becomes cheaper, Bob, it won't come about so it will shorten stopover right away." He stopped, feeling a little sorry for Dahl. "It won't be too bad. There'll be new men up here and you'll pass a lot of time getting to know them."

"Well, you see," Dahl started, "that's why I came back early. I wanted to see you about stopover. It's that—well, I'll put it this way." He seemed to be groping for an easy way to say what he wanted to. "I'm engaged back home. Really nice girl, Chap, you'd like her if you knew her." He fumbled in his pocket and found a photograph and put it on the desk. "That's a picture of Alice, taken at a picnic we were on together." Chapman didn't look. "She—we—expected to be married when I got back. I never told her about stopover, Chap. She thinks I'll be home tomorrow. I kept thinking, hoping, that maybe somehow—"

He was fumbling it badly, Chapman thought.

"You wanted to trade places with me, didn't you, Bob? You thought I might stay for stopover again, in your place?"

It hurt to look in Dahl's eyes. They were the eyes of a man who was trying desperately to stop what he was about to do, but just couldn't help himself.

"Well, yes, more or less. Oh, God, Chap, I know you want to go home! But I couldn't ask any of the others; you were the only one who could, the only one who was qualified!"

*

Dahl looked as though he was going to be sick. Chapman tried to recall all he knew about him. Dahl, Robert. Good mathematician. Graduate from one of the Ivy League schools. Father was a manufacturer of stoves or something.

It still didn't add, not quite. "You know I don't like it here

15

any more than you do," Chapman said slowly. "I may have commitments at home, too. What made you think I would change my mind?"

Dahl took the plunge. "Well, you see," he started eagerly, too far gone to remember such a thing as pride, "you know my father's pretty well fixed. We would make it worth your while, Chap." He was feverish. "It would mean eighteen more months, Chap, but they'd be well-paid months!"

Chapman felt tired. The good feeling he had about going home was slowly evaporating.

"If you have any report to make, I think you had better get at it," he cut in, keeping all the harshness he felt out of his voice. "It'll be too late after the relief ship leaves. It'll be easier to give the captain your report than try to radio it back to Earth from here."

He felt sorrier for Dahl than he could ever remember having felt for anybody. Long after going home, Dahl would remember this.

It would eat at him like a cancer.

Cowardice is the one thing for which no man ever forgives himself.

*

Donley was eating a sandwich and looking out the port, so, naturally, he saw the ship first. "Well, whaddya know!" he shouted. "We got company!" He dashed for his suit. Dowden and Bening piled after him and all three started for the lock.

Chapman was standing in front of it. "Check your suits," he said softly. "Just be sure to check."

"Oh, what the hell, Chap!" Donley started angrily. Then he shut up and went over his suit. He got to his tank and turned white. Empty. It was only half a mile to the relief rocket, so somebody would probably have got to him in time, but.... He bit his lips and got a full tank.

THE RELUCTANT HEROES

Chapman and Klein watched them dash across the pumice, making the tremendous leaps they used to read about in the Sunday supplements. The port of the rocket had opened and tiny figures were climbing down the ladder. The small figures from the bunker reached them and did a short jig of welcome. Then the figures linked arms and started back. Chapman noticed one—it was probably Donley—pat the ship affectionately before he started back.

They were in the lock and the air pumped in and then they were in the bunker, taking off their suits. The newcomers were impressed and solemn, very much aware of the tremendous responsibility that rested on their shoulders. Like Donley and Klein and the members of the Second group had been when they had landed. Like Chapman had been in the First.

Donley and the others were all over them.

*

How was it back on Earth? Who had won the series? Was so-and-so still teaching at the university? What was the international situation?

Was the sky still blue, was the grass still green, did the leaves still turn color in the autumn, did people still love and cry and were there still people who didn't know what an atom was and didn't give a damn?

Chapman had gone through it all before. But was Ginny still Ginny?

Some of the men in the Third had their luggage with them. One of them—a husky, red-faced kid named Williams—was opening a box about a foot square and six inches deep. Chapman watched him curiously.

"Well, I'll be damned!" Klein said. "Hey, guys, look what we've got here!"

Chapman and the others crowded around and suddenly Donley leaned over and took a deep breath. In the box, covering a thick layer of ordinary dirt, was a plot of grass. They looked at it, awed. Klein put out his hand and laid it on top of the grass.

"I like the feel of it," he said simply.

Chapman cut off a single blade with his fingernail and put it between his lips. It had been years since he had seen grass and had the luxury of walking on it and lying on its cool thickness during those sultry summer nights when it was too hot to sleep indoors.

Williams blushed. "I thought we could spare a little water for it and maybe use the ultraviolet lamp on it some of the time. Couldn't help but bring it along; it seemed sort of like a symbol...." He looked embarrassed.

Chapman sympathized. If he had had any sense, he'd have tried to smuggle something like that up to the Moon instead of his phonograph.

"That's valuable grass," Dahl said sharply. "Do you realize that at current freight rates up here, it's worth about ten dollars a blade?"

Williams looked stricken and somebody said, "Oh, shut up, Dahl."

One of the men separated from the group and came over to Chapman. He held out his hand and said, "My name's Eberlein. Captain of the relief ship. I understand you're in charge here?"

Chapman nodded and shook hands. They hadn't had a captain on the First ship. Just a pilot and crew. Eberlein looked every inch a captain, too. Craggy face, gray hair, the firm chin of a man who was sure of himself.

"You might say I'm in charge here," Chapman said.

"Well, look, Mr. Chapman, is there any place where we can talk together privately?"

They walked over to one corner of the bunker. "This is about as private as we can get, captain," Chapman said. "What's on your mind?"

*

Eberlein found a packing crate and made himself comfortable. He looked at Chapman.

"I've always wanted to meet the man who's spent more time here than anybody else," he began.

"I'm sure you wanted to see me for more reasons than just curiosity."

Eberlein took out a pack of cigarets. "Mind if I smoke?"

Chapman jerked a thumb toward Dahl. "Ask him. He's in charge now."

The captain didn't bother. He put the pack away. "You know we have big plans for the station," he said.

"I hadn't heard of them."

"Oh, yes, *big plans*. They're working on unmanned, open-side rockets now that could carry cargo and sheet steel for more bunkers like this. Enable us to enlarge the unit, have a series of bunkers all linked together. Make good laboratories and living quarters for you people." His eyes swept the room. "Have a little privacy for a change."

Chapman nodded. "They could use a little privacy up here."

The captain noticed the pronoun. "Well, that's one of the reasons why I wanted to talk to you, Chapman. The Commission talked it over and they'd like to see you stay. They feel if they're going to enlarge it, add more bunkers and have more men up here, that a man of practical experience should be running things. They figure that you're the only man who's capable and who's had the experience."

The captain vaguely felt the approach was all wrong.

"Is that all?"

Eberlein was ill at ease. "Naturally you'd be paid well. I don't imagine any man would like being here all the time. They're prepared to double your salary—maybe even a bonus in addition—and let you have full charge. You'd be Director of the Luna Laboratories."

All this and a title too, Chapman thought.

"That's it?" Chapman asked.

Eberlein frowned. "Well, the Commission said they'd be willing to consider anything else you had in mind, if it was more money or...."

"The answer is no," Chapman said. "I'm not interested in more money for staying because I'm not interested in staying. Money can't buy it, captain. I'm sorry, but I'm afraid that you'd have to stay up here to appreciate that.

"Bob Dahl is staying for stopover. If there's something important about the project or impending changes, perhaps you'd better tell him before you go."

He walked away.

*

Chapman held the letter in both hands, but the paper still shook. The others had left the bunker, the men of the Second taking those of the Third in hand to show them the machinery and apparatus that was outside, point out the deadly blisters underneath the pumice covering, and show them how to keep out of the Sun and how to watch their air supply.

He was glad he was alone. He felt something trickle down his face and tasted salt on his lips.

The mail had been distributed and he had saved his latest letter until the others had left so he could read it in privacy. It was a short letter, very short.

It started: "Dear Joel: This isn't going to be a nice letter, but I thought it best that you should know before you came home."

There was more to it, but he hadn't even needed to read it to know what it said. It wasn't original, of course. Women who change their minds weren't exactly an innovation, either.

He crumpled the paper and held a match to it and watched it

burn on the steel floor.

Three years had been a long time. It was too long a time to keep loving a man who was a quarter of a million miles away. She could look up in the night sky when she was out with somebody else now and tell him how she had once been engaged to the Man in the Moon.

It would make good conversation. It would be funny. A joke.

He got up and walked over to his phonograph and put the record on. The somewhat scratchy voice sang as if nothing had happened

Way Back Home by Al Lewis.

The record caught and started repeating the last line.

He hadn't actually wanted to play it. It had been an automatic response. He had played it lots of times before when he had thought of Earth. Of going home.

He crossed over and threw the record across the bunker and watched it shatter on the steel wall and the pieces fall to the floor.

The others came back in the bunker and the men of the Second started grabbing their bags and few belongings and getting ready to leave. Dahl sat in a corner, a peculiar expression on his face. He looked as if he wanted to cry and yet still felt that the occasion was one for rejoicing.

Chapman walked over to him. "Get your stuff and leave with the others, Dahl." His voice was quiet and hard.

Dahl looked up, opened his mouth to say something, and then shut up. Donley and Bening and Dowden were already in the airlock, ready to leave. Klein caught the conversation and came over. He gripped Chapman's arm.

"What the hell's going on, Chap? Get your bag and let's go. I know just the bistro to throw a whing-ding when we get—"

"I'm not going back," Chapman said.

Klein looked annoyed, not believing him. "Come on, what's

the matter with you? You suddenly decide you don't like the blue sky and trees and stuff? Let's go!"

The men in the lock were looking at them questioningly. Some members of the Third looked embarrassed, like outsiders caught in a family argument.

"Look, Julius, I'm not going back," Chapman repeated dully. "I haven't anything to go back for."

"You're doing a much braver thing than you may think," a voice cut in. It belonged to Eberlein.

Chapman looked at him. Eberlein flushed, then turned and walked-stiffly to the lock to join the others.

Just before the inner door of the lock shut, they could hear Chapman, his hands on his hips, breaking in the Third on how to be happy and stay healthy on the Moon. His voice was ragged and strained and sounded like a top-sergeant's.

*

Dahl and Eberlein stood in the outer port of the relief ship, staring back at the research bunker. It was half hidden in the shadows of a rocky overhang that protected it from meteorites.

"They kidded him a lot this morning," Dahl said. "They said he had found a home on the Moon."

"If we had stayed an hour or so more, he might have changed his mind and left, after all," Eberlein mused, his face a thoughtful mask behind his air helmet.

"I offered him money," Dahl said painfully. "I was a coward and I offered him money to stay in my place." His face was bitter and full of disgust for himself.

Eberlein turned to him quickly and automatically told him the right thing.

"We're all cowards once in a while," he said earnestly. "But your offer of money had nothing to do with his staying. He stayed because he had to stay, because we made him stay."

"I don't understand," Dahl said.

THE RELUCTANT HEROES

"Chapman had a lot to go home for. He was engaged to be married." Dahl winced. "We got her to write him a letter breaking it off. We knew it meant that he lost one of his main reasons for wanting to go back. I think, perhaps, that he still would have left if we had stayed and argued him into going. But we left before he could change his mind."

"That—was a lousy thing to do!"

"We had no choice. We didn't use it except as a last resort."

"I don't know of any girl who would have done such a thing, no matter what your reasons, if she was in love with a guy like Chapman," Dahl said.

"There was only one who would have," Eberlein agreed. "Ginny Dixon. She understood what we were trying to tell her. She had to; her brother had died up here."

"Why was Chapman so important?" Dahl burst out. "What could he have done that I couldn't have done—would have done if I had had any guts?"

"Perhaps you could have," Eberlein said. "But I doubt it. I don't think there were many men who could have. And we couldn't take the chance. Chapman knows how to live on the Moon. He's like a trapper who's spent all his time in the forests and knows it like the palm of his hand. He never makes mistakes, he never fails to check things. And he isn't a scientist. He would never become so preoccupied with research that he'd fail to make checks. And he can watch out for those who do make mistakes. Ginny understood that all too well."

"How did you know all this about Chapman?" Dahl asked.

"The men in the First told us some of it. And we had our own observer with you here. Bening kept us pretty well informed."

*

Eberlein stared at the bunker thoughtfully.

"It costs a lot of money to send ships up here and establish a colony. It will cost a lot to expand it. And with that kind of

23

investment, you don't take chances. You have to have the best men for the job. You get them even if they don't want to do it."

He gestured at the small, blotchy globe of blue and green that was the Earth, riding high in the black sky.

"You remember what it was like five years ago, Dahl? Nations at each other's throats, re-arming to the teeth? It isn't that way now. We've got the one lead that nobody can duplicate or catch up on. Nobody has our technical background. I know, this isn't a military base. But it could become one."

He paused.

"But these aren't even the most important reasons, Dahl. We're at the beginnings of space travel, the first bare, feeble start. If this base on the Moon succeeds, the whole human race will be Outward Bound." He waved at the stars. "You have your choice—a frontier that lies in the stars, or a psychotic little world that tries and fails and spends its time and talents trying to find better methods of suicide.

"With a choice like that, Dahl, you can't let it fail. And personal lives and viewpoints are expendable. But it's got to be that way. There's too much at stake."

Eberlein hesitated a moment and when he started again, it was on a different track. "You're an odd bunch of guys, you and the others in the groups, Dahl. Damn few of you come up for the glamor, I know. None of you like it and none of you are really enthusiastic about it. You were all reluctant to come in the first place, for the most part. You're a bunch of pretty reluctant heroes, Dahl."

The captain nodded soberly at the bunker. "I, personally, don't feel happy about that. I don't like having to mess up other people's lives. I hope I won't have to again. Maybe somehow, someway, this one can be patched up. We'll try to."

He started the mechanism that closed the port of the rocket. His face was a study of regret and helplessness. He was thinking

THE RELUCTANT HEROES

of a future that, despite what he had told Dahl, wasn't quite real to him.

"I feel like a cheap son of a bitch," Eberlein said.

*

The very young man said, "Do they actually care where they send us? Do they actually care what we think?"

The older man got up and walked to the window. The bunkers and towers and squat buildings of the research colony glinted in the sunlight. The colony had come a long way; it housed several thousands now.

The Sun was just rising for the long morning and farther down shadows stabbed across the crater floor. Tycho was by far the most beautiful of the craters, he thought.

It was nice to know that the very young man was going to miss it. It had taken the older man quite a long time to get to like it. But that was to be expected—he hadn't been on the Moon.

"I would say so," he said. "They were cruel, that way, at the start. But then they had to be. The goal was too important. And they made up for it as soon as they could. It didn't take them too long to remember the men who had traded their future for the stars."

The very young man said, "Did you actually think of it that way when you first came up here?"

The older man thought for a minute. "No," he admitted. "No, we didn't. Most of us were strictly play-for-pay men. The Commission wanted men who wouldn't fall apart when the glamor wore off and there was nothing left but privation and hard work and loneliness. The men who fell for the glamor were all right for quick trips, but not for an eighteen-month stay in a research bunker. So the Commission offered high salaries and we reluctantly took the jobs. Oh, there was the idea behind the project, the vision the Commission had in mind. But it took a while for that to grow."

A woman came in the room just then, bearing a tray with glasses on it. The older man took one and said, "Your mother and I were notified yesterday that you had been chosen to go. We would like to see you go, but of course the final decision is up to you."

He sipped his drink and turned to his wife: "It has its privations, but in the long run we've never regretted it, have we, Ginny?"